FOR RITA, MY MOM

Published in the United States by North-South Books Inc., New York. Published simultaneously in Great Britain, Canada, Australia,
and New Zealand in 2003 by North-South Books, an imprint of Nord-Süd Verlag AG, Gossau Zürich, Switzerland.
Library of Congress Cataloging-in-Publication Data is available. The CIP catalogue record for this book is available from The British Library.
Printed in Malaysia. ISBN 0-7358-1762-6 (trade edition) 10 9 8 7 6 5 4 3 2 1   ISBN 0-7358-1763-4 (library edition) 10 9 8 7 6 5 4 3 2 1
For more information about our books, and the authors and artists who create them, visit our web site: www.northsouth.com

Maybe, My Baby

Marilyn Janovitz

A CHESHIRE STUDIO BOOK

NORTH-SOUTH BOOKS / NEW YORK / LONDON

Maybe, my baby,
if I hold your hand,

Maybe, my baby,
if I warm your toes,

Maybe, my baby,

if I rub your tummy,

Maybe, my baby,
if I nuzzle your chin,

Maybe, my baby,
if I whisper in your ear,

Maybe, my baby,
if I smooth your hair,

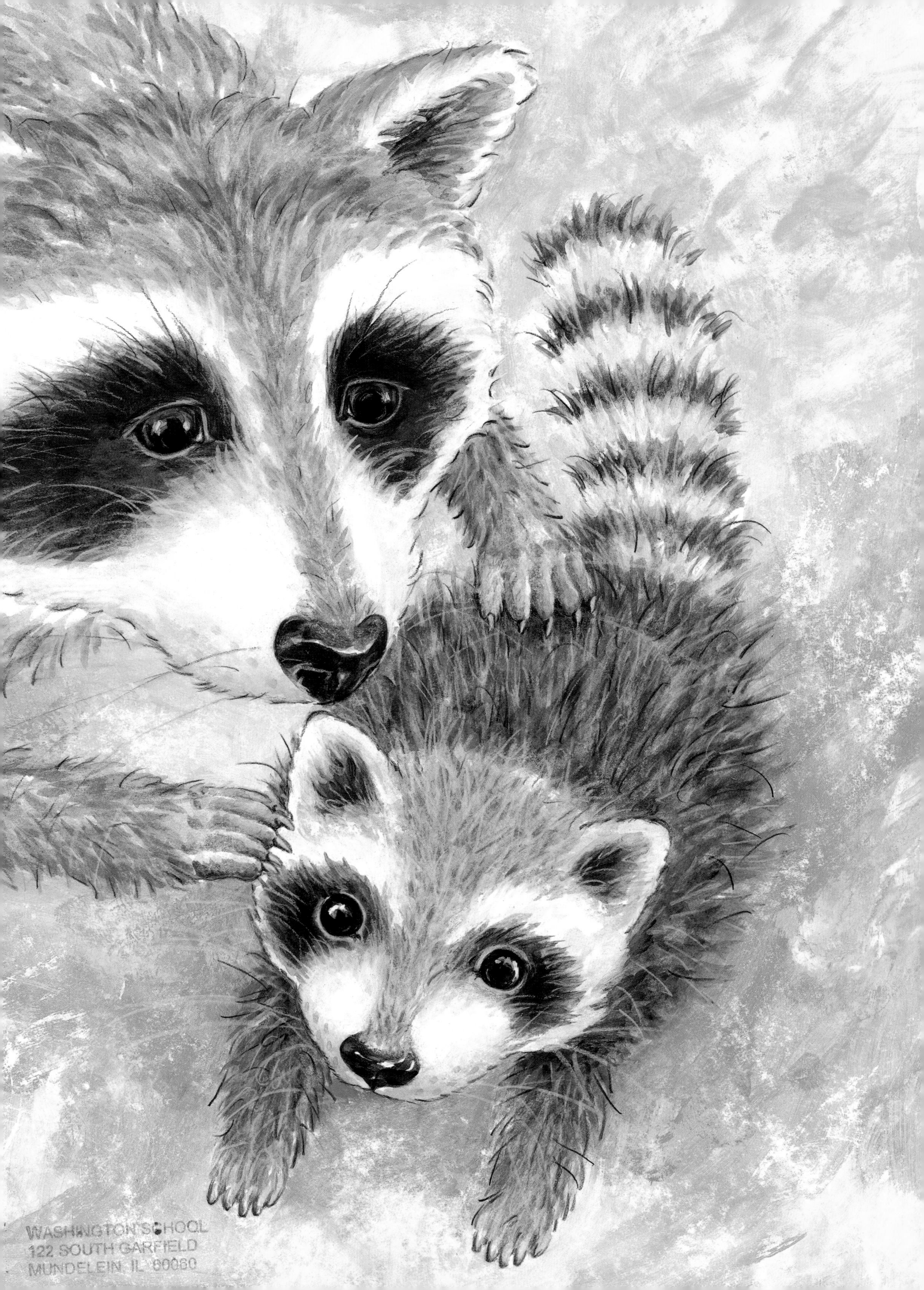

Maybe, my baby,
if I stroke your cheek,

Maybe, my baby,
if I cuddle your neck,

Maybe, my baby,

if I kiss your nose,

Maybe, my baby,
you'll close your eyes,

And maybe, my baby,
you'll fall fast asleep.

Good night, my baby,

good night.